The Winchester Connection

Margaret Scariano

A **PERSPECTIVES** BOOK

Academic Therapy Publications

Novato, Califo

Art Supervisor: Herb Heidinger
Cover Design and Illustrations: Joe Wallace

International Standard Book Number: 0-87879-314-3

1 0 9 8 7 6 5 4 3 2
4 3 2 1 0 9 8 7 6 5

Contents

Contents

CHAPTER 1

The Loser

Hank Mowatt parked his truck in the employees' lot. He hurried along the path to the entrance. His shift as guide began at nine-thirty. Mrs. Corret was the manager of the Winchester Mystery House. She liked the guides to arrive by nine. She always found something for them to do—sweep around the grounds or empty the trash cans.

Hank passed the gift shop. It was near the main entry hall. He hoped Wilbur Rowe wouldn't see him. Wilbur was manager of the gift shop.

"Hey, there! If it isn't our loser. How many tourists you going to leave behind today, Hank?" Wilbur Rowe's laugh sounded as mean as his words.

"Aw, back off, Wilbur, will you?" Hank would like to punch his lights out. Wilbur just wouldn't forget the first day Hank guided a tour. That was when he and his eleven tourists got lost. But Winchester House had one hundred and sixty rooms, secret stairways, and twisting halls. It was easy to get mixed up. It had been Wilbur who had found Hank and his group. Wilbur never forgot. Since then he teased Hank every chance he got.

Hank hurried to Mrs. Corret's office. Wilbur called after him, "Sure you can find your way, Loser? You'd get lost in a closet, I bet." His laugh trailed Hank down the hall like a bad smell.

When Hank entered the office, he could barely see Mrs. Corret. She stood behind stacks of books and piles of papers on her desk. Pencils, two dirty coffee cups, and a box of tissues littered the desk.

"Good morning, Mrs. Corret."

"Oh, is it that time already?" Mrs. Corret peeked around a corner of the stack of books. Her red hair looked like a curly, rag mop. "Find a pencil, Hank, and write these orders down. Keeping that gift shop stocked is like filling a strainer with water. I just ordered *The Winchester Mystery Tour* paperback last week. Or was it two weeks ago? Anyway, Wilbur says he needs more."

Wilbur must be eating them, Hank thought. Just last Thursday he'd ordered four dozen paperbacks for Wilbur's shop.

"Hank, pay attention. I just said order twelve dozen tour books. You're such a daydreamer. Why can't you be more like Wilbur?"

More like Wilbur, Hank thought. No way. I'd rather be a daydreamer or a loser than be like Wilbur. Wilbur loved to play mean tricks. Like jumping out from behind a door and scaring people. Once he whispered through the old intercom, "I know what you did and I'm going to tell." His voice trailed off spookily. The guides and the tourists had been scared. They thought one of Mrs. Winchester's "spirits" was spying. Well, no point in thinking about that guy. Time to get to work.

Hank enjoyed his job as guide. He liked telling the tourists about the mystery house. But he worried. With all the nooks and crannies, it would be easy to lose track of someone.

"Hank, did you write that order down?"

"Yes, Mrs. Corret. Twelve dozen tour books."

CHAPTER 2

Someone's Missing

It was almost ten. One of the guides poked his head in the office. "Mrs. Corret, we got lots of people waiting for a tour. Could Hank help us now?"

"Run along, Hank. And thanks." Mrs. Corret ducked behind the stack of books.

Hank went quickly to the entrance. The tourists stood around waiting for a tour. "Good morning," he said. "I'm Hank Mowatt. I'll be your guide through this house of mystery. Mrs. Winchester died in 1922. It took the moving people six weeks to move the furniture out because they kept getting lost. So let's count off. I don't want to lose any of you."

The people smiled as they counted. "One, two, three . . . "

"Fourteen of you. Let's hope the same number returns." Hank turned and headed toward the curving stairway. "Please stay together. Parts of this house are unsafe. I don't want any of you to fall through a trap door. If you have any questions, I'll try to answer them as we go along."

Hank stopped at the foot of the stairs. "In 1884, Mrs. Winchester bought this house in San Jose, California. It had eight rooms. In 38 years she added 152 rooms. So it now has 160 rooms. Did you see the porch and stair posts? They are all upside down. Why? Some think it was to trick the spirits—the souls of those killed by the famous Winchester rifle. This rifle was invented by Sarah Winchester's father-in-law.

The house has strange features. You will see that the number 13 is in many of the patterns. There are 13 panels on the ceiling, 13 windows in many rooms, 13 hangers in the closets. The light fixtures have 13 bulbs. There are 40 stairways in the house. Most have 13 steps. There are also, you guessed it, 13 bathrooms." Hank started up the stairs.

"This Winchester lady must have been a real nut," one of the tourists mumbled.

Hank stopped half-way up the stairs. He turned to face the tourist. "Mrs. Winchester certainly was not a nut. Perhaps a little strange. Maybe lonely. She lost her baby daughter and her husband. But she wasn't a nut. She spoke four languages. She was a musician and an architect. She gave lots of money to charity. Her gifts were never made public. In memory of her husband she gave more than a million dollars to a hospital." Hank started up the stairs again. It made him mad when visitors made ugly remarks about a lady they didn't even know. "Follow me. I'll point out some of her ideas."

They stood in one of the many halls. Windows stretched from one end to the other. "See, these window locks are made like the Winchester rifle trigger," Hank said. "You see, Mrs. Winchester believed that death would never come as long as she kept building on her house. So carpenters pounded away for 38 years."

One of the tourists put his hands over his ears. "Noises like hammers and saws keep spirits away. Is that why she had a seance room?"

Before Hank could answer, the young girl spoke up. "Mrs. Winchester used sand between the floors which deadened the sound."

That girl acted as if she were the guide. Hank took over. "Mrs. Winchester also used rock wool to insulate her house." He stepped closer to the window. "She invented an inside crank to open and close windows. Later you'll see a fireplace with the first hinged iron drop for ashes."

The group moved to a bedroom. The young girl tugged at Hank's sleeve. "You didn't mention the hidden wood boxes," she said.

"Have you been on the tour before?" Hank asked.

"No, but I read. And so you see, I know." She walked away.

And so I see, Hank thought, you're a know-it-all.

Hank led his group through the strange house. They climbed two-inch stairs that led only to the ceiling. They opened doors to blank walls. They saw cupboard doors with no cupboard space behind them. Hank showed them the Grand Ballroom. It had been built without a single nail.

His final talk took place on the main floor in front of the Tiffany doors. Hank said, "Notice the leaded glass windows. They're not flat like church windows. They are wavy. Some of the 'bull's eyes' in the windows are really optical lenses. If you look through them, the view is upside down. These large doors were opened only three times during the time Mrs. Winchester lived here. They opened the last time for Mrs. Winchester's coffin. This ends the tour. But before you leave, let me count to be sure you are all here. We started with fourteen."

Hank counted. Thirteen. Was the girl missing? No, she stood by the entrance to the gift shop. Hank counted again. There were only thirteen tourists now. Someone was missing.

There were only thirteen tourists now. Someone was missing.

CHAPTER 3

The Search

Hank's heart pounded. He rubbed his sweaty palms on his pants. Was someone playing a trick on him — someone like Wilbur Rowe? Not funny. Maybe he'd missed someone. He counted the group again. Thirteen. No more, no less. Already he could hear Wilbur's laugh. "Lost another tourist? You're a regular loser, Hank." But maybe one of them had gone to the restroom.

Hank asked, "Did any of you see someone drop out or stay behind?"

The tourists shook their heads. "No," they all said.

"Well, do any of you know who's missing? Are all husbands and wives together? Do you have all your children?" Hank tried to keep his voice low, but he was getting scared.

The tourists looked around. All husbands and

wives and children were present. Hank began to sweat. How could he lose a person? He had stayed close as they moved from room to room. How?

"Please look around," he said. "Do you remember seeing anyone who started the tour who isn't here now?"

Silence. Everyone looked at everyone else. Then one woman said, "There was a man. I don't see him now. I remember him because he wore beads that tinkled like bells."

"Oh, yeah," another tourist spoke up. "I remember him. He mumbled under his breath a lot, too."

"Was he with anyone in this group?" Hank asked. He began to remember the man with the beads. He was a little bald.

The tourists all shook their heads.

"Don't you think you should get a description?" the young girl asked. She stood next to Hank now. A notebook and pencil were in her hand.

"Sure. I was just going to do that," Hank said.

He asked the tourists to tell what they remembered about the missing man. The young girl wrote down what they said. Then Hank told the tourists they could go. He read the list.

People were funny. The tourists agreed that the man was a male. But that was all. The rest sounded like thirteen different men. Some said he was about five and a half feet tall with black curly hair and beads around his neck. Others said he was six feet and bald and wore a medal on a chain. Another said there were no beads and no medal. One man said he wore a print shirt. Another said he wore a sweater.

"This doesn't make any sense," Hank said. "Nobody agrees. The missing man is tall, short, or in between. He is in his late twenties or early sixties." In disgust Hank crumpled the paper.

"It does tell us something," the young girl said. "For example, the tourists agree he isn't a teenager. And so you see . . . "

"And," Hank broke in, "it's time I report this. Thanks for your help." Hank rushed down the hall to Mrs. Corret's office.

"Lost?" Mrs. Corret asked. "Oh, no! How could you lose a full-sized man? Find him. Get going!"

Beads of sweat dotted Hank's forehead. He felt cold fear in the pit of his stomach. He wanted to run down the hall and yell, "Come out. Come out. Wherever you are." He forced himself to walk fast but not run. As he passed the other guides, he asked, "Hey, do you have an extra guy on your tour?"

One guide stopped and counted. "Nope. Still got just nine. What's the matter? You lose another one, Hank?"

"Yeah. Thought I was keeping them together, but some guy wandered off."

Hank asked another guide in one of the thirteen bathrooms. No luck!

One tourist grumbled to his wife. "Corn, Mabel. This is pure corn. Hokey. That's what it is. Stirring us up about a missing tourist. It's all part of the act."

"Try the storeroom, Hank," the guide said. "People always like looking at all that stuff."

Hank did, but no one was there. By this time Hank had questioned all five of the guides. Where could that guy be? Maybe Winchester House has a ghost, Hank thought.

CHAPTER 4

Someone's Found

Mrs. Corret told Hank to skip his next tour and keep searching. "Look in the garden area. Look around the statue of Chief Little Faun. There are a lot of bushes there. A good hiding place. Tourists love that little Indian with his bow drawn against the Winchester rifle. Then cover the four floors of the house right to the attic. Don't forget the Blue Seance Room. You might even look in the greenhouse on the second floor. Even though it's supposed to be locked. Now, go!"

He went inside the house and checked out the spook's barroom. No one was there. Next he went to the ballroom just off the front hall. He thought about the words of his tour talk: "Weekly dances were held here, but not for people. Mrs. Winchester put on her finest dress and entertained spirit visitors. She danced with her ghostly guests." No time to think about that now. Where was that guy?

Then he remembered the greenhouse room. Mrs. Winchester had kept her indoor plants and flowers there. But the room was still off limits to tourists. Fire extinguishers hadn't been put in there yet.

He took a key from his ring of keys. He unlocked the door and stepped inside. He looked around quickly. No one. Another dead end. Then he saw the legs. They dangled from a large tub. It looked like someone bobbing for apples.

Hank felt sick. What a way to end a tour. Had the man fainted and fallen in? Hank had to pull the man's head from the tub. "Hey, Mister, you all right?" he called out.

No answer. Hank's knees shook. He gulped. Slowly Hank tiptoed toward the tub. There was something familiar about the man's brown denim pants and the high-topped work shoes. A copy of *The Winchester Mystery Tour* paperback stuck out of the man's back pocket. Hank took the book out so when he turned the man over, he wouldn't be lying on it. How silly! What does that matter if he's dead!

Maybe he could give him first-aid. Get him breathing. He grabbed the man's shoulder to turn him face up. He saw the black and blue finger marks on his neck.

Hank twisted the body over in the tub and looked into the man's face. He'd found him, all right. But it wasn't the missing tourist.

Then he saw the legs. They dangled from a large tub.

15

CHAPTER 5

Meet the Brain

Hank couldn't believe it. But it was true. The man was Joe Ming, the gardener for the Winchester Mystery House. Poor Joe. He's always been nice to me, Hank thought. When I lost my first group of tourists, Joe didn't tease me. He just patted my shoulder. He said, "Hank, don't mind Wilbur. He's a mean man who hasn't had his mistakes found out yet."

Hank looked again at Joe. Should he check for a pulse? But where? Was it in the wrist or in the neck? He felt both. Nothing.

"No point checking his pulse with your thumb."

Hank jumped. There in the doorway stood the young girl from his tour. She walked over to Joe Ming and looked into his face. She touched his wrist with her two fingers.

She explained. "The thumb has a pulse. And

so you see, you never take a pulse with it."

"Is he alive?" Hank asked.

"Of course. But I don't know how badly he's hurt. His skin is cold." The girl wore braces on her teeth that looked like a cage. She nodded. "So you can see he has been choked and is in shock."

"Shock. Who wouldn't be? Say, how do you know about all that stuff?" Hank asked.

"Science is my bag. I've made a study of the effect of shock on rats."

"Mr. Ming isn't a rat. And this is no place for you. You'd better stop a guide and follow his tour out of the house. I don't want anyone else to get lost." Hank thought this girl was something else. 'Made a study on rats . . . ' Boy!

She looked at him. "Lost? Hardly. I know perfectly well where I am at all times. It's a matter of the sun and . . . "

"Beat it, kid," Hank said.

"I believe you are going to need me. Otherwise, how are you going to get this man out of the tub? Or do you plan to just leave him?"

"Leave him?" She'd been working with rats too long, Hank thought. "Well, my knees have stopped shaking. Let's lift Mr. Ming from the tub. If you'll grab his legs, I'll hold his head and shoulders. We'll lay him out alongside the tub."

Hank looked quickly at Mr. Ming. He looked so gray. Hank shut his eyes. "On the count of three, lift. OK?"

Together they lifted Joe Ming and stretched him out on the floor. Hank picked up *The Winchester Mystery Tour* paperback to put beside him. As he did so, a note fell out of its pages. It floated to the floor. Hank bent down to pick it up. "Gosh! It's a note to someone. Listen." He read: "I will wait no longer. Pay up. Or I go to the police. In the greenhouse room at eleven. TODAY."

"This is clearly a case of blackmail," the Brain said. She took off her sweater and laid it across Joe Ming.

"Blackmail?" Hank asked. A shiver ran down his spine.

The Brain nodded. "A classic case, Hank."

Hank had to give her credit. She was so smart. He put the note in his pocket. Then he knelt down beside Joe Ming again. "How does he look to you now?"

"His skin is still bluish. Let's put something under his head. It shouldn't be lower than his feet." She looked around the room. Nothing that could be used as a pillow. She put her purse under his head. "This will prop him up enough."

Joe Ming's eyelids fluttered. He moaned.

"Well, at least we know he's still alive," Hank said.

The girl put her fingers on Joe Ming's neck. "His pulse is stronger now, too."

"You sure know a lot about injuries. Are you going to be a nurse or something?" Hank asked.

"No. Let me introduce myself. I am Carla Collins. Most people just call me the Brain. Who are you?"

"Hank. Hank Mowatt." He didn't mention that some people like Wilbur Rowe, called him "Loser." "Glad to meet you, Brain." He stopped a moment. "Say, you weren't wearing all that stuff in your mouth on the tour, were you?"

"No. I must wear these braces three hours a day. I plan to visit the library at 4:00 today. I can get my three hours in before then." She looked at her wrist watch. "At exactly five minutes after three I can remove this." She pointed to the wires covering her mouth.

"I know you won't forget," Hank said. "You probably never forget anything."

"You're right. I have programmed my mind. It will alert me at five minutes after three." She grinned, adding, "But just in case, I also have the alarm on my wrist watch." Then she turned serious. "Now, Hank. Who is this man and what is he doing here?"

"Joe Ming. He's one of the gardeners at the Winchester House. He has a small apartment in back of the hot dog stand. I haven't any idea why he's up here."

"Think, Hank. Joe Ming is a gardener. This room is a greenhouse. So you can see he was here on gardening business."

This kid was something else. Hank felt like laughing. He didn't want to hurt her feelings. She was so serious. Hank explained, "You're right about this being a greenhouse, but there's no planting done here now. Joe Ming didn't have any reason to be here. Except maybe that note." Then he added "Maybe we should get help for Mr. Ming. Is it all right to leave him?"

"He's breathing normally now," the Brain said. "Let's go."

"I have to tell Mrs. Corret too. And who knows? Maybe the missing tourist has turned up by now."

CHAPTER 6

The Blue Room

The Brain followed Hank out of the greenhouse. They turned to head down the hall toward the stairs. Then Hank saw a man at the end of the hallway. He was alone. No tour was around.

"Look. Bet that's our missing tourist. He just ducked down that hall."

Hank and the Brain dashed after the man. As they turned the corner, a guide with a group of tourists was coming toward them.

"Did you pass a man just now?" Hank asked.

"Yeah. I thought he was one of the janitors."

"Do me a favor, will you?" Hank asked the guide. "Get a hold of Mrs. Corret right away. Tell her to call an ambulance. Oh, yes, and the police. Someone tried to choke Joe Ming. He's in the greenhouse room."

Hank heard gasps from the tourists. One of them said, "Guide, take us out of this place.

Right now. We don't want to be involved with the police."

The group began to mutter and talk. The guide held up his hand. "Just a moment, please." He turned to Hank. "You're not putting me on, are you?"

"No. Hurry!" Hank pushed by the tourists with the Brain right behind him.

"What happened?" The guide called after them.

"I'll explain later." Hank and the Brain rushed down the long hall. But now the hallway ahead of them was empty.

"Where did he go?" the Brain asked.

"He's got to be in one of these rooms. The stairway is behind us. We know he didn't pass us. We'll just have to check each room."

They opened door after door. One door opened to an elevator. Hank said, "Mrs. Winchester used this elevator to carry her plants to the greenhouse." Another door was just a door with a wall behind it. There was a glass door to a bathroom.

"That's kind of strange, isn't it?" the Brain asked.

"Yes. Most of the bathroom doors are glass. Some people say they were put in so Mrs.

Winchester could keep her eye on the servants. Others say it was so the maids could watch her in case she fell. She was not strong for many years before she died."

"That makes sense," the Brain said.

"Come on. We're wasting time," said Hank. "Let's find that tourist."

They walked down the hallway together. "He's got to be in one of these rooms," Hank said. "There's no other way down." Then they heard the noise. A humming sound. Or was it more like chanting?

"Brain, it's coming from the seance room." They tiptoed up to the door and listened.

"Ommmmm. Ommmmm. Ommmmm."

Hank looked at the Brain. Her eyes were wide. She looked scared. "I don't believe in spirits, Hank. But that noise. It doesn't sound like it's coming from this world."

"There are two of us. And that missing tourist didn't look too big when we saw him in the hallway. We can handle him," Hank said. He sounded braver than he felt. Somewhere he'd heard that people under a "spell" had great strength. Well, he had no choice. Brain wouldn't stay here by herself while he ran for help. And he didn't blame her a bit. He didn't want to be left alone either.

"Is it true that Mrs. Winchester kept this room locked at all times? Did she really put on special robes and talk with the spirits in there at night?" the Brain asked.

"You're stalling, Brain. Are you going to help me or not?" Hank asked.

"Of course. I just want to prepare myself for what's ahead." She closed her eyes. She took a deep breath and held it for a moment. She let it out and opened her eyes. "There. I've got all the fear out of my mind. I am ready for what's ahead."

Hank, with Brain right behind him, opened the door. They stepped inside the Blue Seance Room. The room was small. It had no windows. The only light came from the open door behind them. There, sitting on the floor, legs crossed, was the missing tourist. He didn't even look up when they came in. His head was thrown back. His arms were stretched out wide. He continued with the strange sound. "Ommmm. Ommmm. Ommmm."

"Hey, there. What are you doing?" Hank stepped forward. He tapped the man on his shoulder.

"Trying to contact my wife in the other world.

Ommmmm."

"Come on, sir. You'll have to get in touch with her someplace else." Hank bent down. He took hold of the man's arm.

The man pulled back. "You don't understand, young man. My wife is here. Expecting me to talk with her. I'm just about ready to make con-

There, sitting on the floor, legs crossed, was the missing tourist.

tact. Ommmmmm."

Brain stepped ahead of Hank. "Sir, maybe your wife is downstairs waiting for you. We'll take you."

"No, she wouldn't be there because she's here. Or almost here. It's her brother. He keeps popping up. No way will my wife's spirit come if her brother's spirit is here. They didn't get along on this earth. It hasn't changed in the Other World. He raised his head toward the ceiling. Ommmmmmmmm."

"Now cut that out!" Hank pulled the man to his feet. "Let's go. You're not supposed to be in here."

"Neither is he. Come here, you!" The missing tourist nodded toward the open door behind Hank and Brain.

"Who?" Hank turned around to the open door. There was no one there.

Hank saw just a flash as the tourist rushed by him, yelling, "Wait. Wait for me. I want to talk to you."

CHAPTER 7

Chase!

Once again Hank and the Brain chased down the hallway after the tourist.

"I think we got him cornered. He's at the end of the hall," the Brain said. "Unless there's another hall leading off this one."

"No. This is just a regular hallway. Ends just about where he's standing," Hank said. He kept up his speed. He really wanted to catch that guy!

But it was a case of now you see him, now you don't. One minute the tourist was at the end of the hall. The next minute it looked as if he'd stepped through the wall. Vanished!

"My eyes saw that man go through a wall. My mind will not accept that. And so you see, I must be dreaming." The Brain stopped and shook her head.

"No, I don't see that at all," Hank answered.

"We couldn't both be dreaming the same dream at the same time. Follow him!" Hank raced down to the spot where they had last seen the tourist.

They reached the end of the hall. Aha! A panel in the wall was shoved aside. Quickly they stepped through the opening. They were on a small landing. Thirteen tiny steps led down to a door.

"Keep moving," Hank said. "I'm right behind you."

"I'm going as fast as I can," the Brain whispered. "And you might be quiet. We don't want to scare the guy off."

Now they were at the door. They turned the knob and stepped into a small room. No tourist!

Hank looked at the Brain. He couldn't believe all of this. She shrugged. She was as puzzled as Hank.

Just then they heard a click. They saw the door at the top of the thirteen steps close. For a moment Hank was stunned. Then he realized what was happening. Someone was locking them in. He rushed back up the steps to the door.

"Wait!" he called. He turned the knob. Nothing. Then he kicked the door and pulled on the knob. He stood there. "Hey, the joke's over. Open up." Surely whoever was playing a trick on them would open the door now and laugh. There was a second sliding sound like a panel being pushed in place. Then silence.

He rattled the knob again. He kicked at the door. He pounded with his fists. "Hey, it's not funny any more," he yelled. "Open up."

"Don't panic, Hank," the Brain said. "A cool head is what is needed. There is a way in and so you see, there is a way out. To put it another way, the tourist came in and went out. And so you see, we came in and we can go out."

"And so you see! See what? I've had it up to here with your 'and so you can see' bit."

"Well, what are we going to do, then?" the Brain asked.

"We could yell. One of the guides might hear us."

"Soundproof. That's why this room has never been found until now."

"If it's soundproof, that means it's air-tight," Hank said.

The Brain beamed. "Good, Hank. Now you're thinking clearly. Very good."

"Very good, huh? Air-tight means no air out. And no air in. We'll suffocate."

CHAPTER 8

Secret Room

Hank had to hand it to the Brain. She had guts. Maybe she was a good bluffer, too.

"Suffocate, Hank? That doesn't make sense. There has to be a way out." She grinned. "You know, we got in and so you see — and all of that."

"Yeah, you're right." Hank smiled at the young girl. No point in laying his fears on her now. He didn't even want to think about *not* finding a way out. He used to catch butterflies when he was a kid. He'd put them in an air-tight jar. They fluttered their wings wildly at first. Finally, with a quiver, they died. No. Suffocation was not a great way to go.

He looked around the small room. It was empty except for four boxes in the corner opposite the door. He walked over to look. At least he'd feel like he was doing something to get them out of this mess.

The Brain was busy, too. She took out her pocket calculator. She paced off the room. Then she tapped some numbers into the computer. "Seven by seven, squared . . . then the wall space should equal . . ." The Brain shook her head. "It just doesn't compute." She mumbled some more numbers and paced off the room again.

Hank kicked at the boxes. They were solid. He took out his pocket knife and slit open one of the boxes. It was filled with *The Winchester Mystery Tour* paperbacks. He opened the other three boxes. They were filled with the same books. Strange, Hank thought. Mrs. Corret said that Wilbur Rowe needed more books for the gift shop. Just this morning he'd placed an order for twelve dozen. But here was a large supply. He reached in the box and took one out. He flipped the pages. A square had been cut out of the middle section. Hank looked at several others. The same cut-out square was in them. Guess these are damaged books, Hank thought. They certainly couldn't be sold.

Once again Hank looked around the dim room. Cobwebs clung to the corners. In the center of one was a large black spider. Hank stepped back. He shuddered. Just then the Brain spotted the web. "Ugh. Another spider. There's a whole nest of them over there." She pointed to the far corner. "They have real long hairy legs and red eyes."

"And so you see," Hank said with a grin.

"And so you see — I don't like them." Her voice shook. "And I don't like my head almost touching the ceiling. I feel like I'm being squashed."

Hank felt the same way. Poor kid. He knew she was scared. He was. His heart was pounding so hard he was sure she could hear it. He said, "Hey, Brain, maybe one of the ceiling panels lift up. You know, like a trap door. Hand me one of those books. I'll use it to poke the ceiling."

The Brain watched while Hank jabbed the book at the ceiling. It was solid. There were no loose panels.

Hank sighed and sat down on the floor. He rested his back against the wall. "I'm sorry, Brain." He felt helpless.

"You tried, Hank. That's what counts. Want to talk about something else?"

"Sure," Hank said. "Nothing to lose. What do you want to talk about?"

"You," the Brain said and smiled. "Is this your first job?"

Hank laughed. "No, I've washed dishes,

delivered newspapers, cut lawns. How about you? Do you baby-sit or something?"

"No." She shook her head. "The baby-sitting business is not for me. First, you're on call. Secondly, the hours keep changing." She grinned. "And then there are the kids. Some are great. But some are really awful! And so you see, I'm in business for myself."

"Don't tell me. Let me guess," Hank said with a grin. "You raise rats."

The Brain laughed. "Nope. I grow bean sprouts for the health food store."

"It figures. You're something else, Brain." In his mind Hank could see her tending her plants.

"Bean sprout farming is great," the Brain said. "I plant in plastic buckets. Then just lay the buckets on their sides. Add water and harvest the sprouts every two weeks."

"No dirt? No weeds?" Hank asked.

"Nope. With my method bean sprouts can be grown the year 'round. Bean sprouts are easy."

Hank looked up at the ceiling. He saw the light with thirteen bulbs hanging low. Even the Brain couldn't walk under it without bumping her head. Hank remembered that Mrs. Winchester had been a tiny woman. She was only four feet, ten inches tall. What did she use this secret room for?

Hank's thoughts were jamming now. If this room were built after the 1906 earthquake, he was sure there would be a way out besides the door. The earthquake had trapped Mrs. Winchester in her bedroom. She had been terrified that might happen again. She wouldn't risk that. The missing tourist had come through the door just the way he and the Brain had. But he'd gone out some other way. Hank knew there had to be another way out. Not only because of the tourist's vanishing act but because of Mrs. Winchester's fears. If only he could find it before they ran out of air!

CHAPTER 9

A Way Out

Hank tried not to let the panic build inside him. He needed a plan of action. Once again he started walking around the room. He felt and tapped the wall panels from top to floor board. Tapping on the third wall, he heard a hollow sound. Hank carefully ran his fingers over the panels from top to bottom. Near the floor board he pressed the wall. The panel slid up slowly and softly. There, behind the wall, was a small plat-form elevator. It was just big enough for the two of them to stand on.

"Brain! I found it. I found the way out!" Hank yelled.

"The Brain punched one more number into her calculator. "Great, Hank." She walked over to the opening. "I'm sure that with a few more calculations, my little computer would have come up with the answer too. "

"Come on, Brain. Who cares? We can get out of here." Hank waited until the Brain stepped on the platform. Then he got on the other side of the rope pulley to balance it. In a few moments they were on their way down a narrow, dark shaft.

"Any idea where this thing stops?" the Brain asked.

Near the floorboard he pressed the wall. The panel slid up slowly and softly.

"Nope. It can go right to China as far as I'm concerned. I'm glad to be out of that room."

The elevator moved downward slowly. Suddenly it stopped. It seemed to hesitate a moment. There was a clicking sound. Hank's heart skipped a beat. But the elevator continued down. With a sharp jolt it touched bottom. Light leaked through the edges of a door. Hank opened it. He stepped into the kitchen. They were on the ground floor. But they still hadn't found the missing tourist. They hurried toward the entrance hall.

In front of the gift shop stood the five guides, some tourists, Mrs. Corret, Wilbur Rowe, and the police. The missing tourist, handcuffed, leaned against the wall. His eyes were closed. "Ommmmmmmm," he chanted.

"Line up, ladies and gentlemen." Mrs. Corret said to the tourists. "Another tour will be starting in just a few minutes." She led the way to the far side of the hall. "Just stand there. A guide will take you through the mystery house in a few minutes."

A stretcher with a blanket covering Joe Ming was near the door. His eyes were closed, but Hank could see him breathing.

Hank and the Brain walked up. "There they

are," one of the guides yelled.

"Good grief! Where have you been, Hank?" Mrs. Corret's voice made everyone grow quiet. Even the "Ommmmms" stopped.

"You're real trouble, Hank." Wilbur Rowe stood behind the counter near the doorway. His smile made Hank think of a snarling dog. Wilbur said, "What's with you anyhow, Hank?"

A man from the group of tourists stepped inside the gift shop. "I'd like a copy of *The Westminister Mystery Tour*," he said.

"We're all out," Wilbur said. "Check back later."

"Again?" Mrs. Corret asked. "I'll phone the order in right away. I just can't keep enough copies of that book in stock."

Hank was puzzled. *Westminister,* the tourist had said, instead of Winchester. Then he remembered the boxes of *The Winchester Mystery Tour* paperbacks in the secret room. It hit him. He knew now why Joe Ming was left for dead.

CHAPTER 10

Who's the Winner?

A few minutes later a teenaged girl walked up to the counter. "May I have a copy of *The Winchester Mystery Tour,* please? And a package of gum, too."

Wilbur reached under the counter. He pulled out a paperback for her. He dropped it and the gum in a sack. "Two dollars and thirty-six cents, Miss."

It computes, as the Brain would say, Hank thought.

Then the ambulance men arrived and took Joe Ming to the hospital. The police told Mrs. Corret that the tours could start again. "We'd like to question these two." The police nodded at Hank and the Brain. "The rest of the guides can go about their business."

Hank and the Brain stood in the doorway of the gift shop. They answered questions. Hank told about the missing tourist. He told about finding Joe Ming hurt in the greenhouse. He told how the Brain and he had followed the tourist into the seance room and then lost him.

"Well, we got him now." The policeman nodded toward the handcuffed tourist. "Guess that's all. We've got your names and addresses in case we need more facts." He pointed to the "Ommmmmming" tourist. "We'll take this guy down to the jail right now and book him for assault."

"What about motive, officer?" the Brain asked. "This tourist has no reason to hurt the gardener. He was just trying to contact his wife's spirit."

"We'll check it out, young lady. Sometimes motive isn't as clear-cut as TV shows seem to show."

"The tourist didn't hurt Joe Ming," Hank said. "He had no reason to. And so you see," Hank looked at the Brain and smiled, "someone else must have done it."

The Brain beamed at him.

Wilbur shook his head. "'Loser' is too good a name for you, Hank." He half-laughed as he turned to the puzzled police. "Take the tourist away. This guy always fouls things up. 'Foul-up

Hank.' That's what you should be called."

"Ommmmmmm." The chant was louder now.

"And a crook is what you should be called, Wilbur." Hank walked behind the counter. "Look," he said to the officer. "The top shelf has regular copies of *The Winchester Mystery Tour*. The lower shelf has copies with a square cut out of the center pages. I think to hold drugs. The key word is whether the customer asks for *Winchester,* the regular tour book, or *Westminster,* the book with the cut-out section filled with drugs." Hank turned to Wilbur. "When Joe Ming blackmailed you about this, you tried to kill him." Then he added, "I bet the finger marks around his neck match yours."

"Tell them about the secret room, Hank," the Brain said.

"Secret room?" Mrs. Corret yelled. "Oh, no! That means we have to do all our brochures over. Not 160 rooms but 161 rooms. What next?" She leaned against the wall limply.

"What a flake you are," Wilbur growled. He began to move toward the door. The policeman stepped in front of him.

There was a loud ringing sound. Mrs. Corret screamed. "Is that a fire alarm? Now what?"

The police placed hands on undrawn

revolvers. Hank jumped.

The chanting tourist stopped 'Ommmmming.' "You must let me go," he said. "That's the spirit signal. I must go. Right now! My wife will be expecting me."

The Brain stood still. Then she turned off the alarm on her wrist watch. "Oops! Five minutes

"What a flake you are," Wilbur growled. He began to move toward the door.

after three," she said. "My brain must be over-loaded. I actually forgot the time." She took the wire from her mouth.

The tourist leaned across the counter and looked at Wilbur carefully. "Aha! There you are. I finally caught up with you. Now once and for all, stay away from my wife's spirit. Hear?"

The policeman looked mixed-up. "What's going on here?"

"He thinks Wilbur is his dead brother-in-law. And the man's wife won't talk to him if her brother-in-law's spirit is around. Or something like that."

"Oh." The policeman looked as if he didn't understand.

Hank turned to the Brain. "You know something, Brain? It wasn't the tourist who locked us in the secret room. It was Wilbur. And it was also Wilbur the tourist saw standing in the doorway of the seance room. I should have figured that out."

"How?" the Brain asked. "We didn't see Wilbur lock us in." Her hands were on her hips. She looked as if she didn't understand.

"It's simple, Brain," Hank said. "It's a matter of not enough time. You see, from the time we got in the secret room until the door was locked took just a few minutes. The tourist didn't have enough time to go in the elevator and then run back up to the second floor."

The Brain grinned. She looked better without the wires on her teeth. "Right, Hank."

"Besides," Hank added. "One of the guides would have seen the tourist. But Wilbur could move around the house. He works here. No one would question him." He paused and took a deep breath. "And so you see, a second person, Wilbur, locked us in the secret room."

The Brain's smile was wide. "Good, Hank. And so you see, your name is no longer 'loser,' but 'winner.'"

The police took the tourist away and Wilbur, too. Hank thought about Joe Ming. Poor guy. He hoped he'd get better soon. What was it he'd said about Wilbur? He had said, "He's a mean man who hasn't had his mistakes found out yet." Well, Wilbur's mistakes were found out now.

"Wilbur is the real loser, Hank," the Brain said.

"Good grief!" Mrs. Corret moaned. "Who will run the gift shop?"

"Me," Hank said.

"In that case," the Brain grinned, "I think I'll buy a book! One copy of *The Winchester Mystery Tour,* please."